BLOW

Blow

by
M. A. Savino

Chapter One
A Night Out

The music inside the club vibrates the floor beneath my feet. I stand in the dimly lit hallway lined with other women in various forms of club wear, waiting to use the bathroom. Colorful dots speckle our faces as the disco ball spins above the dance floor.

My sister, dressed in a skin-tight red tube top dress, dances with an unfamiliar face. I told her to stay at our table until I came back from the bathroom, but as usual, she didn't listen. The ladies' room door slams open, and two girls in matching silver dresses stagger out, knocking me into the wall on their way past me. I roll my eyes, glance back at the dance floor, and scan the crowd for my sister. She waves from the far side of the dance floor as she jumps up and down to the music, spilling more of her drink than drinking it. I wave back and push the bathroom door open.

There are only three stalls, and of course, one of them is out of order. I push open the door to the first stall. Feces, blood, and piss overflow onto the floor with piles of sopping wet toilet paper stuffed inside the toilet bowl.

The other stall is occupied, so I lean against the sink, and moisture seeps into my cream dress pants. I turn around, peering at the wet spot in the mirror over my shoulder. My face drops, and I gag as a yellow stain spreads across the ass of my pants.

Fuck this place.

I don't even get why this club is so popular. People like coming here to dance, and so do I, but it's disgusting.

The stall door opens, and a petite red-haired girl stands beside me. When I turn to enter the stall, she says, "It's out of toilet paper, hun."

My thighs inadvertently tighten. I've been holding my pee for an hour already, and I'm seconds away from squatting in the alleyway. The redhead unzips her purse and removes a little pack of tissues. "Here, use these," she says with a pearly white smile.

"Thank you," I say, accepting the tissues and entering the stall. I reach for the slide lock on the back of the door, and it falls to the ground and skids under the stall door. "Oh, for fuck's sake," I say as I push and hold the door closed with one hand and hold the top of my pants after pulling them down with the other, trying not to let them touch the floor.

Once I've emptied the multiple drinks that filled my bladder, I release the unsecured door and wipe with the tissues the redhead provided.

I wash my hands and throw the bathroom door open, the music growing louder. In the corner of my eye, I catch a glimpse of a red dress pressing through two men in the crowd before disappearing in a sea of dancing bodies. Rachel is nowhere near our table. When I catch up to her, I'm dragging her from this pit and getting the fuck out of here.

The music quiets briefly as one song jumps to another, and a crowd of dancers yell out to the booming bass of a familiar song. My head starts to pound, the music becoming too loud, the air around me growing thick with the scent of beer on breaths and marijuana baked into the fabric of their clothes. My feet slip in various fluids spilled carelessly on the floor as I search for Rachel. Having a little sister is sometimes more trouble than it's worth. I catch another glimpse of a red dress, this time going into the club's smaller bathroom beside the bar.

There she is.

An audible huff moves the long blonde hair of the girl blocking my path. She peers over her shoulder at me, her eyes glossy and bloodshot, the front of her black mini skirt revealing every piece of lint, fabric, and fiber.

"Excuse me," I roar over the blaring tunes.

Her thick eyebrows elevate right before she turns her body aside and extends her hand to the path in front of her. "Oh, no. Excuse me, your highness," she says, slurring her words.

I don't bother thanking her. It's not like she'd remember anyway. The bathroom door slams open, and a girl exits wearing a dress nearly identical to Rachel's. From behind, I can't tell the difference. Even her long brown hair is similar to my sister's, leaving me dumbfounded. I quickly turn around and let my eyes land on every stitch of red I can see. It's everywhere now, much like when you're searching for a specific car model and color on the road, and suddenly, they're everywhere.

But none of them is Rachel.

I quickly check our table and find her black sweater still hanging over the chair. Blood rushes to my face, rage overwhelming me. She knows better. I shove my way toward the DJ, who sits on a higher elevated platform, pushing men and women aside on my way to the front. Vulgar names and expletives launch from multiple patrons' mouths as I become frantic and desperate to find her. As I ascend the three steps to the DJ booth, a bouncer places his tribal tattooed hand on my shoulder, stopping me from entering. I've danced with him a few times before so it's not like he doesn't know who I am, but he has to do his job. I shout into his ear that I lost my sister and need to find her. He nods and waves me into the booth. The DJ holds his headphones to one ear and spins a record, not noticing me standing there, caught up in the beats. I wave my hand in front of his face, and he turns to me. "Yeah?" he shouts, turning his exposed ear toward me.

I cup my hands around my mouth, allowing my words to flow directly into his eardrum. "I need to find my sister, Rachel. She's somewhere in here, but I can't find her, and we need to go."

The DJ nods. "And your name is?"

"Olivia."

He turns the volume of the music down and brings the microphone to his lips, hushing the booing from the crowd. "Now listen up. We have Olivia up here looking for her sister, Rachel. Rachel, please come to the DJ booth."

I mouth a quick thank you as the DJ turns the music back up, and I stand on the steps beside the bouncer, waiting for her to break through the sea of people crowding the dance floor like ants on a sidewalk. A pit grows in my stomach as a minute, then two, then five ticks by. I glance over my shoulder at the bouncer, who shrugs.

Something's wrong. I descend the steps, my head spinning as I search the crowd, rushing to each bathroom and throwing every stall door open, even the out-of-order ones. I quickly return to the DJ booth, snatch the mic from his grasp and yell, "Everyone, listen up please. I need to find my sister. Can you please stop what you are doing and look around you? She's wearing a red tube top dress. She has long brown hair and brown eyes. Her name is Rachel."

The mic grows heavy in my hand as the crowd shrugs off my words. The DJ takes the mic from my hands and returns to his turntable. I exit the stage and search every make-out spot, every face, and every corner of the club, but she's not here.

Where is my sister?

Chapter Two
The Vanishing

I call her multiple times, but she doesn't answer.

I wait. Maybe she stepped out to pull money from a nearby ATM and will be back shortly.

I reason. Perhaps she's left and headed home without me. No, she wouldn't do that.

All the calling, waiting, reasoning, and searching yield no results. She's not here. She's nowhere.

As the hours pass, I watch the faces of every partier exit the club until finally it's just me and the bouncer. I don't know his name, despite our repeated dance encounters. He's eyed me from the DJ booth on several other occasions, so I think he might want to be more than dance partners.

"Did you find her?" he asks, stopping in front of me.

I can't talk, let alone breathe. She's my responsibility, and I lost her. He glances over my shoulder and shakes his head at someone standing behind me. When I turn around, the DJ closes the door on his van, sealing his equipment inside with a quick beep of his fob.

The lights of the bar darken, and the neon sign flicks from open to closed.

"Maybe she left," the bouncer says as he turns back to face me and smiles with reassuring blue eyes.

"No, she'd never leave without telling me where she was going," I yell, making him take a step back and put his hands up.

"Okay," he says, wiping his palm on the front of his tight black shirt before stuffing his hand in his pocket. "Do you want me to wait with you while you call someone? You really shouldn't be out here alone."

I nod, rubbing the chill off my arms as the night turns cold. Or maybe it's the bad feeling I have, draining the blood from my body, turning my tan flesh pale and clammy.

Lights and sirens flash in front of an alley a block away. It sits just within eyeshot where I can see the darkness of its passage, flashlights lighting up its graffiti-covered grim brick walls.

I step away from the bouncer, cautiously moving toward the flashing lights, mesmerized by their pattern as they draw me closer to them. As I close in, an officer unrolls yellow crime scene tape across the entrance to the alley, ripping the end of the roll with his teeth. I break away from the bouncer, kicking off my heels and sprinting as fast as my feet can carry me, pavement gliding beneath my bare feet. I slide sideways around the corner, snapping the yellow barrier as I enter the opening of the alley. My eyes widen when I see the red dress lying on the ground. The air around me thickens, and my stomach and throat tighten. I scream and push past an onlooker recording the scene on his cell phone. "Rachel!"

An officer leaps in front of me, trying to stop me from getting to her. I slap his hands away. Another officer reaches for me, and I dodge him, too.

My legs slam into the pavement at her feet, tearing open the knees of my pants, and blood seeps into the fabric.

Foam bubbles around her mouth and white powder litters the space beneath her nose. A blood-curdling scream comes from somewhere unknown. I wrap my arms around her lifeless body and hold her. "No!"

A paramedic rests his arm on my shoulder and applies a gentle pressure, trying to pull me away from her, but I hold on tight, tighter than I ever have.

"I'm sorry. She's gone," he murmurs solemnly.

I can't believe what he's saying to me. Why is he giving up so quickly? I've seen this on many Live PD episodes, so if he won't give her another dose, I will.

"No. You hit her again," I order, letting Rachel go and grabbing at the zipper of the medic's bag. "Give her another dose of Narcan." I frantically yank the zipper open, my hands blindly fumbling through his bag.

The medic wraps his hand around my wrist, gently removing it from his bag before zipping it back up and resting his hand on mine. "It won't help. We found her too late."

His eyes, kind and soft, cast pity upon me before he glances over his shoulder at the officer standing behind him and shakes his head.

I fall into Rachel's lap, the weight of my sorrow making it impossible to move. A flashlight reflects off a small plastic baggie lying next to her hand with a black rose on its face.

My sister doesn't do drugs. She never has. She has always been the wholesome child of the family. Someone must have coerced her, forced her to take it, tricked her even. Tattooed hands wrap around my waist, lifting me away from her. I kick and thrash my body, trying to break free from the bouncer's grasp. He lowers me slowly to the ground without letting me go, holding me tight against his chest as I bawl, the heartache raw and burning a hole through my chest. His massive hand encapsulates my face, keeping me from looking at her as the police collect the envelope of remaining drugs from beside her. The bouncer turns me away, combing my hair with his fingers as he walks me, staggering at his side, out of the alleyway.

People crowd the alley exit, including the man with the phone recording when I first arrived, now live-streaming about what's happened.

Before I have a chance to react, the bouncer yanks the phone from the man's hand and smashes it on the ground, shattering its screen. "Have some respect," he yells before ushering me onto the sidewalk.

My legs, weakened by shock and grief, fail me, and I fall to the sidewalk, landing on my knees.

A whimper escapes my lips as the bouncer kneels beside me. "Tell me what I can do?"

There's nothing he can do. There's nothing anyone can do to stop the flood of rage, sadness and regret surging through my veins. An officer approaches, a small notebook in his hand. The sound of nearby traffic grows louder in my ears, grabbing all of my attention.

An emptiness takes over as my heart shatters at the thought of having to tell our parents. The tears stop flowing, and a sudden calmness releases the weight holding me on the cold, hard concrete of the sidewalk. I stagger to my feet, the bouncer giving me space but staying close as I search my surroundings, suddenly aware of how lonely I feel. I'm lost without her. She's my best friend, was my best friend, and someone killed her.

A drop of rain lands hard on my cheek, then another as the rain becomes steady, washing away the salty white streaks on my face. I don't want to be here anymore. Facing my family is a worse punishment than death. I turn toward the bouncer, studying his face briefly before realizing that even he can't stop what happens next.

A silver sedan barrels through the traffic light when it turns green, and my feet move on their own, carrying me into the center of the road, where I close my eyes and let fate decide.

Chapter Three
Helpless

A beeping sound filters in my ears, distant at first, but slowly grows louder as I wake. There's no one here with me—my parents, friends, no one. I'm alone, lying in a hospital bed, my leg wrapped in a cast from just below my knee down to my toes.

The smell of flowers wafts into my nostrils, drawing my eyes to the bedside table beside me. A card sticks out from between long stems of red roses, pink carnations, and white baby's breath. On the front is a simple message and phone number.

Call me.

Jobie
Club Beats

Jobie must be the bouncer.

I close my eyes, and flashbacks of Rachel flood my mind. The memory of her pale, lifeless face, the plastic baggie with a black rose ink stamped on it, and the medic's hand resting on mine sends a wave of sadness through me.

Someone killed her—killed my only sister and best friend with their tainted drugs. Tears spill over my lids, and I blink them away as I glance back at the table beside my bed. Beside Jobie's bouquet, daffodils with white carnations sit inside a yellow vase with a black smiley face. The card dangling around its neck lifts the hairs on the back of my neck.

Sorry for your loss.

There's no signature, just the message. Who the fuck would send a happy bouquet? I stretch my arm to the table, just reaching the notecard with my fingertips, and tug it closer to me. The stretch band snaps off the vase with a quick yank of my wrist. I flip it over, checking the back for a signature.

The card crumples in my hand, bending a black rose someone ink-stamped on the back of it. The one who drugged and killed Rachel had to have sent them. Who else could it be? But why? To taunt me? Or is it a twisted apology like they are saying "sorry, not sorry" I drop the card beside me, wrap my hand around the vase and launch it with all my might across the room. It slams into the wall, shattering by the door, just missing the gray-haired nurse rolling in the blood pressure cart.

"Jesus." She jumps back out of the room, holding her hand on her heart. She peers down the hall to her left. "We need housekeeping in here."

As she enters the room, I look away and stare out the window, watching a butterfly fluttering on the sill. Rachel loved butterflies.

Fresh tears well and fall onto my lap as the nurse wraps the blood pressure cuff around my bicep, and it tightens around my arm. "It's nice to see you finally awake. You've been sleeping for over thirty hours. Part of that's the anesthesia and, of course, grief, but now that you're awake, we can take that catheter out and get you something to eat and drink."

"I don't want anything," I say with a heavy sigh without looking at her. The butterfly hovers outside for another minute before it changes course and disappears.

"She's saying goodbye," the nurse says as she walks away from me and leans on the wall near the window. "But it's not forever. You'll see each other again someday."

I furrow my brow and send the nurse a questioning look.

"The police were here." She tilts her head and closes her eyes with a relaxed smile, letting the afternoon sun's heat warm her face. "I told them to come back later." Her eyes spring open, and she turns to me. "You need time to mourn your sister before they burden you with questions."

A terrible pain in my chest doubles me over, and my body trembles uncontrollably. The bed sinks beside me as the nurse sits down and takes my hand. "It wasn't your fault."

I clutch my chest, the sharpness inside it, threatening to tear me apart as I nod and say, "Yes, it is."

She squeezes my hand tighter, the veins in her hands stretching. "No, dear. You can't control what other people do."

"I should have been with her, right by her side. But I left her alone. I might as well have killed her myself."

The nurse releases my hand and stands. "Now you listen here, young lady, the only person responsible for your sister's death is the person who put the drugs in her hands." She bends over and picks the card from the smiley face flowers off the floor, studying it front and back. "Was this with the flowers you tried to kill me with?"

I take it from between her red painted nails, rip it in half, and say, "Just throw it away."

She opens her palm, and I drop the pieces inside as a man with black-framed glasses and greasy jet-black hair enters the room, carrying a broom and dustpan.

"Listen." She pats my arm after removing the blood pressure cuff. "I'm here all day. If you need anything, just let me know."

I manage a small smile for her kindness. It's the best I can do under the circumstances. The glass scrapes against the floor tile as the housekeeper sweeps it slowly into the pan and dumps it in the trash can. He scoops the flowers up and carries them to my table, his hand clutching the stems just over the vase Jobie bought me.

"What are you doing?" I say, pulling my table closer to me and away from him.

His eyes dart to me, then the flowers and back again before saying, "I thought you might want to keep the flowers; there's plenty of room in this other vase for them."

I shake my head. "No. I don't want those flowers. Please take them with you."

"All of them?" he asks, picking up Jobie's vase as well.

"No!" I shout, pointing to the yellow and white bouquet from the killer. "Just take those."

The man pushes his glasses up the bridge of his nose. "Why?"

Heat surges through my body, sending flames through my veins straight to my mouth as I yell, "Because they are from my sister's fucking killer."

Chapter Four
Stewing

A knock on the wall directs our attention to the door. My father stands in the doorway, his eyes bloodshot and red from crying. I've never seen him cry. Ever.

He's a tough guy who believes men who cry are pussies. My sister's sudden death has hit him hard, and I find it difficult to look at him. The janitor squeezes past him as I stare down at my fingers, chipping the blue nail polish from their tips, a tear dripping onto my cheek out of nowhere.

His hand rests gently on my head and strokes my hair with a tenderness I don't deserve. "Hey, kiddo."

My eyes stay fixed on the flecks of paint on my lap as I say, "I'm sorry, Daddy."

He wraps his arms around me, crushing me in his grasp. Our sobbing starts quietly and gradually increases in volume as we grieve for Rachel. "It's not your fault, Liv."

Ever since I was a toddler, my dad has called me Liv. The only time he called me Olivia was if I was in trouble.

"Where's Mom?" I ask, pulling away from him.

After a few heartbeats of silence, he finally says, "Making the arrangements." His voice cracks, and he chokes on his words. "She'll probably be by later."

Probably.

That's the only word that stood out to me in that statement. Rachel was my mom's favorite. Parents can say they don't have favorites, but the truth is, we always connect more with one than the other. I have always been Daddy's girl, and my sister was my mom's. It never bothered either of us that our parents had a preference. Now, my mother has lost Rachel, which, to me, will create a divide between us.

"Liv?" My dad touches my arm to get my attention, and I finally look at him. I mean, really study his face—his eyes, his heartache, his sorrow. It matches mine, but there's something else. Something emanates from us both that I recognize as only one thing.

Rage.

Another trait my dad and I share is the ability to feel each other's emotions. He wants the person who did this to Rachel to die just as severely as I do, but he would never act on it; he has too much to lose.

I, on the other hand, have already begun hatching a plan. Of course, it will have to wait until after the cast comes off.

It all starts with the club. Someone there must have seen something or knows something. I turn to my dad, take his hand in mine, and ask, "Did anyone find Rachel's phone?"

He nods. "The police have it."

A nurse appears across the hall and presses four buttons on the locked medication room.

Beep, beep, beep, beep.

"They said it was cocaine mixed with fentanyl." His voice trails off, blending into the background. "Did you hear me?" My dad asks, his voice becomes clearer as my mind wanders back into the room.

I glance at him, dry the moisture from my face and say, "I'm going to find her killer."

He shakes his head and squeezes my hand tight. "Liv, the police said it was an overdose, and that there were no signs someone forced your sister into taking anything."

My hand slides away from his. "Dad, you know Rachel. She'd never try drugs. How can you even believe that?"

"Honey, I didn't say I believe it. I said it's what they're saying."

Beep, beep, beep, beep.

Another nurse enters the med room.

"I don't care what they say. Someone gave her those drugs, someone put them to her nose, and someone made her take them. And when I get out of this cast, I'm going to find out who." I cross my arms as both nurses exit the med room, cackling like a couple of school girls who just shared a juicy secret.

The fluorescent light above me hums louder as the sudden silence between my dad and I speaks volumes. He knows my temper and how protective I've always been of my little sister. Once, when I was in eighth grade, a bully pushed Rachel at the bus stop, and I punched him. My knuckles not only hit the bully's cheek, they sideswiped his friend beside him, wiping the smug smile off his face and knocking both of them to the ground. After that, kids at school called me Muhammad after the great boxer. My mom wasn't happy with me, but my dad took me aside and told me he was proud of me for watching out for my sister. It's too bad I wasn't there for her this time when she needed me the most.

"I called your work and let them know you'll be out for at least a month," he says quietly. "They're going to put your time in as vacation now, so you'll get it with your next check and can pay your bills."

Well, that's one less thing I'll need to worry about, I think to myself as a figure appears in the doorway.

My father stands as Jobie, the bouncer from Club Beats, enters the room and extends his hand to him. They shake hands as if they've already met and exchange pleasantries before my dad turns to me, kisses me on the cheek and says, "I'll be back in a bit."

I watch him leave as another nurse enters the med closet.

Beep, beep, beep, beep.

Jobie sits in the chair that my dad just left. It scrapes against the tile as he scoots closer and asks, "How are you?"

How am I? Is he joking?

"What are you doing here?" I ask, not answering his question.

He rests his elbows on the edge of my mattress and rubs his face with his palms. "You freaking almost died. What were you thinking?"

"I asked you a question, Jobie. What are you doing here?"

His eyes flit to mine. "I don't know."

"Bullshit." He barely knows me, and he's left flowers, exchanged handshakes with my dad, and now sits next to my bed. "If you can't be honest, then fucking leave," I say, turning my attention to the setting sun outside.

A heavy sigh from his lips shifts the fine hair on my arms before he says, "I'm sorry. I'm sorry about your sister, I'm sorry I couldn't stop you from running into the street, I'm sorry if my being here upsets you." He looks away from me and stares at the floor, rubbing his palms together between his legs.

He's nervous.

When his eyes leave the floor and meet mine, he says, "And if you want complete honesty, I'm also here because if you had died, I could have never asked you out on a date."

"Jesus Christ," I murmur. "Are you using my sister's death and my accident to get me in bed?"

His eyes widen. "Of course not. What kind of person do you think I am?"

"I don't know who you are," I say sternly before looking away from him. "I don't even know who I am anymore." I gaze out the window. The sky, now casting off colors of pink mixed with purple and hints of blue, darkens further, and I can't look away from it as I say, "It's my fault." My voice quivers. "And I'm going to make it right."

"Look at me, Liv," Jobie says, his voice deep and gritty.

My head snaps in his direction as blood rushes to my face. "Don't call me Liv. Only my parents and sister call me that." I clench my fists. "Leave."

He nods and rests his callused palm on my arm as he stands. "This wasn't your fault, Olivia."

I yank my arm away from him and point toward the door. "Get out of my fucking room, Jobie." Tears sting my eyes, burning their way down my cheeks as I shove him backward with one hand, feeling the firmness of his muscular abdomen. "I said, get the fuck out!"

He hangs his head, and his eyes lock on the trash can beside my bed. His knees crack as he kneels beside me and lifts the torn card from the killer from my garbage, pushes the two pieces together and stares at it. "Where did this come from?"

My words come out quiet and defeated. "Just go." I'm so tired. All I want is to close my eyes and sleep until this nightmare comes to an end.

Jobie seizes my arm suddenly, startling me and taking my breath away as he holds the pieces of torn paper with the black rose on it in front of my face and says, "Olivia, where the fuck did this come from?"

My mouth opens, but only staggering gibberish escapes my lips. His sudden concern sends my stomach into a frenzy, and my heart pounds hard in my chest. There's a desperation in his eyes I can't ignore, and suddenly I don't feel safe. He almost looks scared, but of what?

"Why?" I finally ask.

He crumples the papers in his grasp, stuffs them in his jeans pocket, turns away from me, and quickly exits the room. I stare at the space where he once stood and wonder why he's so upset. The same nurse who has been in the med closet before punches her number into the panel.

1-1-1-4

Beep, beep, beep, beep.

A young blonde girl enters my room, carrying a tray of food. She sets it on the table beside me, pushes it over my lap, and then removes the top. "Do you need anything else?"

I shake my head at the gravy-covered turkey and mashed potatoes that I won't be eating. As she walks through the door, I pick up the cup of coffee and pop its plastic lid. I haven't had a cup of coffee or anything besides water for two days. My appetite is nonexistent, but my mouth is so dry.

A wheelchair bangs against the doorway, and Jobie barrels into the room, startling me and sending coffee across the top of my hand. I wince as it burns my skin and hover it before my lips, blowing the steam floating above it gently. Before I get a single drop of the black liquid energy, Jobie snatches the coffee away from me, spilling more on my hand, and says, "Don't fucking drink that."

"What the hell are you doing?" I ask as I rub the red mark on my flesh.

He thrusts the table away from my lap, sending the tray of food flying across it. It lands on the floor with a loud bang as he tosses my covers off me and stares down at the catheter still taped to my leg. "Fuck," he murmurs.

His finger frantically presses the call button, beckoning the nurse to come to my room.

She rounds the corner and presses the cancel button on the wall before saying, "You don't have to press it so many times. Once will suffice. Now what do you need?"

"Take the catheter and IV out. We are leaving, right now."

I gawk at him, towering over the nurse, his eyes demanding and his sharp jaw set.

The nurse peers over at me and says, "Well, you haven't been discharged, and there's paperwork and such to do."

"No!" Jobie shouts, making the nurse jump. "She has to leave now. Get her the 'Against Medical Advice' papers or whatever."

My face prickles and my body trembles as I realize something is very wrong. I don't know what it is, but Jobie seems genuinely concerned for my safety, and even though I don't know him, I find myself trusting him with my life. "Take out my IV and catheter. I want to leave," I say to the nurse.

She crosses her arms and frowns. "Well, you have to sign paperwork, and maybe you should have your father take you."

As she turns to leave, I grab the side of her scrubs and pull her back to me. "I'm twenty-one years old. I decide when I leave this hospital. Now, take the shit out of me, or I'll do it myself."

She stares down at my hand, tightly gripping the fabric of her pants, and says, "Fine."

I release her pants, and she works quickly to remove the catheter and IV Jobie bites the side of his thumbnail as he rocks back and forth on his heels. A piece of gauze and white medical tape slaps over the hole in my hand, and the nurse says, "I hope you know what you're doing."

The second she's out of the way, Jobie leans over me and says, "I'm going to transfer you to the wheelchair."

His hands press beneath my back and under my knees, and he lifts me effortlessly into the seat. The footrests clank down, and he takes my sock-covered feet one by one and sets them in the footrests. His eyes trace a line from my only exposed calf up to my gown, barely covering the goosebumps on my thigh. He yanks the blanket from the bed and gingerly covers me before saying. "You're coming home with me."

I gasp, my mind racing. What the hell is going on? "What? I can't go home with you, I don't have any clothes, and you're a stranger."

He stands, walks to the back of the wheelchair, and grips the handles. "I'm Jobie; you're Olivia. There, we've officially met and are no longer strangers. I'll get your clothes later." He pushes me quickly through the door and walks briskly to the elevator. "Besides, you can't stay at your place alone. Who will take care of you?"

He has a point. I didn't think about how I'd get around once I made it to my place. But having a guy I just met take care of me was the last thing I would have thought of.

His palm slaps the down button repeatedly, and as the doors close us in, I gaze over my shoulder at him and say,

"Why are you taking me? What's really going on?"

He stares straight ahead, appearing to be deep in thought as the elevator whooshes down to the first floor. I wave my hand over my head, and he blinks several times before looking down at me. "I have to take you somewhere safe," he says as the elevator door pops open.

"Safe from who?" I ask as the wheelchair bounces over the threshold of the hospital exit.

The wind blows my hair across my face as he pushes me across the parking lot at Mach speed. I grip the arms of the wheelchair tight as we bounce over a pothole, and my ass lifts off the seat before slamming back down, sending a sharp pain through my spine. "Jesus, Jobie. Slow the fuck down," I yell over my shoulder.

He continues ignoring me as we weave between cars. When I peer up at him, his head is on a swivel, scanning the area around us every few seconds. His paranoia melts into me, and my entire body trembles—fear of an unknown foe spreading through me like a virus.

We pull beside a midnight blue SUV with tinted windows. He opens the front passenger door, hoists me into the seat, and yanks the seatbelt around me, clicking it into place.

I snatch his hand, gripping it tight, and ask again, "Jobie, safe from who?"

He studies my face as if he's seeing me for the first time. His hand plunges into his front pocket, and he pulls out the crumpled card pieces with the black rose on it. He tosses them onto my lap and says, "From them."

Chapter Five
Awkward

Thirty minutes later, Jobie's third-floor apartment door swings open, revealing nothing but pitch black. He walks effortlessly through the darkness and sets me down. I sink deep into a plush couch as the lamp beside me flicks on, blinding me momentarily. The apartment is not only spotless, it's massive and not at all what I expected from a club bouncer.

Jobie kneels at my feet, lifts my cast leg, and rests it on a pillow on the coffee table. "Comfortable?"

"Yes, thank you. But…"

He holds his pointer finger between us and presses it firmly against my lips. "Hold that thought."

I sit still, mouth dropping wide open, wanting to ask for—no, demand an explanation, but he leaves the room quickly. My fingers glide across the velvety couch, leaving a mark where my hand was in the fabric. The thick carpet beneath my foot seeps between my toes. Everything about his place is luxurious, from the rug to the fixtures; even the kitchen counters appear to be of the highest quality. Bouncing can't be his only job. Not in this city.

A blanket floats over me, startling me at first as Jobie shakes it into my lap before smoothing it around my hips. He flops into the black leather chair across from me, rests an elbow on its arm, and rubs his bottom lip with his thumb. "Can I get you anything?" he asks, leaning forward and resting his elbows on his knees.

"Answers would be fucking great," I say, my eyes unwavering.

He blows out a heavy sigh and says, "The flowers, the notecard, they are a direct threat to your life."

I recoil my neck, my words staggering from my lips. "My life? Why? I don't understand."

He slides off his chair and sits beside me on the sofa, resting his arm on the back of the couch behind me. "Your sister's death has drawn the attention of the police to a very dangerous group of individuals. If they even think you saw something or have a photo on your phone or if there's one on Rachel's, you're in danger."

His glossy eyes stay locked on mine, emanating a darkness from them I can't put my finger on. "How do you know all this?" I ask.

He removes his arm from behind me and says, "It's my job as a bouncer to keep club patrons safe, including you."

I frown and say, "Well, you did a shitty job. My sister's dead."

He hangs his head and interlaces his fingers on his lap. When he looks back at me, regret shines bright in his eyes. "If I weren't stationed at the DJ booth, yes, Rachel may still be alive, but that isn't even a guarantee."

"I want to go home." I pull the blanket across my lap and gaze down at my clenched fists. It's not like I can do anything about my current situation. I'm wearing a hospital gown, and a heavy cast inhibits my ability to walk, let alone run away if I wanted to. Going home may not be the best idea under the circumstances.

Amusement shines bright in his eyes as he turns his body to face me and says, "Listen, I have your dad's number. He gave it to me when you were being evaluated. I can call him and let him know you are here with me and safe. Will that make you feel better?"

"*Feel better*? You basically just told me someone may want me dead. No matter who you call or what you say, nothing is going to make me *feel better*." I do need to find the guy Rachel was dancing with. He's the key to finding out what happened, so maybe that's something Jobie can help with.

"I'm sorry," Jobie says softly, resting his palm on my still clenched fist. "Is there anything I can do to help you through this?"

I turn my head slowly to face him, my eyes brimming with fresh tears. "You can find out the name of the man my sister was dancing with, for starters. I saw the club has cameras. As a bouncer, I'm sure you have access."

His hand slides off mine, and he rests it on his knee before pushing himself to a stand.

"Liv, it's not that easy. If I go poking around asking questions and wanting to review surveillance, word could get back to The Reaper."

"The Reaper? Is that the gang's name that uses the rose symbol?" I ask, sitting up taller in my seat. The more information I can get out of him now, the less I'll have to find out on my own later when my leg heals.

He walks away from me and stands by the window, placing his palms high on its frame as he exhales slowly. "The Reaper isn't a gang, it's a person." He pushes off the frame and stalks toward me. "And you'll never get to him."

I press my palms into the couch cushions and lean toward him as he squats in front of me. "And why is that?"

I flinch as he reaches for my face. He hesitates briefly before plucking a strand of loose hair from my cheek and says, "Because, Liv, no one knows who he is."

My fingertips sting as I slap his hand away from my face. "I told you, don't call me Liv." I scan the area around the sofa.

"Didn't you grab the crutches from my room?"

He shakes his head, a small smile of amusement playing on his lips. "Nope." His body towers over me as he stands, blocking the light and casting a shadow over me. "You're stuck here with me."

I sit forward in my seat, launch myself to a stand and immediately tip backward. His arms wrap tightly around me, stopping me from falling back to the sofa cushion. He holds me there tight, close, trapped, and says, "You aren't going anywhere."

A squeal escapes me as he lifts me quickly off the ground and carries me toward a partially closed door. He pushes the partition open with the tip of his boot, revealing a well-lit bedroom with a king-size bed in its center.

"What the hell are you doing?" I ask, my eyes flitting from him to the bed and back again.

"Not that," he says, thoroughly amused by my assumption.

My hands slide across the red silk comforter as he sets me down gently and says, "You'll be safe here."

He exits the room, leaving the door open. I scan the white brick walls, filled with massive abstract paintings. To my right, an enormous window provides a view of the city in the distance, and another window sits kitty-corner from that one. I swing my legs off the bed, put all my weight on my good leg, and hop to the big window. Down below, the busy street is lit up with the head and taillights of hurried drivers as they speed down the roadway. I hop to my right and gaze at the brick side of another building. Below me is an alleyway with a massive dumpster.

"There's no way down," Jobie says, entering the room with a black round plate in one hand and a bottle of water in the other. He sets them on the nightstand beside the bed and slides his hands in his pockets. "Turkey and provolone on rye with lettuce, tomato and Dijon mustard. The chips are freshly made at a deli down the street." He turns away from me and places his hand on the doorknob. "This is for your own good."

Before I can ask what, the door closes and an audible click follows, followed by the unmistakable slide of a deadbolt securing me inside.

"No," I say more to myself than to the closed door.

I plant my hand on the wall and use it to scale across to the door. I pound on it with my fist and yell, "Jobie, I know you didn't just lock me in here." I grip the handle and turn, but it doesn't budge. "Jobie?" My voice cracks as he doesn't answer, and panic sets in.

He fucking locked me in his bedroom. Oh, wait until my dad finds out. I hop back to the window just in time to see Jobie staring up at me from the street, a playful smirk on his lips. He thinks this is funny. Let's see how funny he thinks this is. I grab the small lamp with a metal base from the table, tap the glass with its bottom and smile down at Jobie. He shakes his head at me as I reel my hand back and smash the pane with the lamp. Nothing happens. Not a crack, not a chip, not even a smudge mark. His bedroom windows aren't made of glass; they are made of ballistic acrylic. What in the actual fuck? Why the hell does he have locks on the outside of his bedroom door and fortified windows? I toss the lamp on the floor, shattering its bulb, and slap my palm against the glass as he presses his palm against his puckered lips and blows me a kiss.

Chapter Six
A Model Prisoner

For the next several weeks, I battled back and forth with Jobie about locking me in his bedroom before he leaves for work. He'd be gone sometimes for over eight hours, and even though there's a bathroom in his bedroom and plenty of space, it feels claustrophobic. He let me talk to my dad a few times while he stood there listening to the conversation, and even when I told my dad Jobie had me locked up, my father didn't seem troubled by it. Jobie must have really told him a great story of how much danger I was in.

I've concluded that no matter what I say, he's not going to let me leave until I'm capable of being on my own. I get it, he seems to care a lot. He dotes on me, serves me meals, and even wraps my leg up for me so I can take baths, but he's never crossed a line.

Today, his unusual silence unnerves me. He carries in a tray, but it's empty when he places it across my lap. I gaze up at him, wondering if I'm starting a fasting diet that I didn't know about. "What's going on?" I ask, staring up at him, his dark eyes hard and determined.

He exits without a word, leaving the door open. When he returns a few moments later, he's carrying an iPad and a manila folder. He presses the power button on the iPad, taps the screen a few times with his pointer finger, and turns it toward me. "Swipe left to go to the next photo and tap to view the video at the end." He drops the iPad and the manila envelope on the tray and says, "I'll be back later."

I stare at his back as he moseys out of the room, closing the door softly behind him. The audible click of the lock twists my stomach in knots as I stare at the items in front of me.

My hand trembles as I pick up the iPad and gawk at the first image. It's Rachel dancing with the mystery man. It appears she took a selfie of them dancing and posted it on social media. As I scroll through the images from Rachel's phone, I wonder how Jobie got access to it. Did they release the phone to my dad, and did he take what he needed off it to create this slideshow just for me? The next several shots are of seemingly unimportant things: the floor, an accident, I'm sure; the bartender shaking up a drink for a man with his back to the camera, wearing a graffiti-covered jacket; Rachel's cleavage; and the partially clean-shaven face of someone standing behind her, possibly the guy she was dancing with. The next photo appears to be a still from a surveillance camera near the dance floor. Jobie is standing on the DJ booth speaking to me on the steps when I first started asking to announce Rachel as missing. I continue scrolling through the images, some with Rachel, some with unfamiliar faces, until I stop at one marked with triple red circles around a dark-haired and bearded face. The man's palm is held in front of the camera as though trying to block the shot, but he is still clearly visible. Jobie is standing just to the side of him. It's not the guy who was dancing with Rachel. It appears to be the guy, based on the hair color and the graffiti jacket, that the bartender was making a drink for in one of the previous photos. The following image, a still from the surveillance camera, shows Jobie speaking to the man Rachel was dancing with at the bar.

I press a file labeled "summary" and read it.

The man dancing with Rachel states that he bought the tainted drugs from the man in the graffiti jacket with the intent to 'loosen her (Rachel) up a bit'. The man in the graffiti jacket claims he "doesn't know what I'm talking about, has never met the guy Rachel was dancing with," and shuts down any further conversation.

There's a side note from Jobie.

The graffiti jacket guy is lying. See footage.

I click the video file, and booming bass music startles me, and I fumble the iPad in my hands, nearly dropping it. I turn the volume down to a level where I can still hear and scan the crowd. I stretch the video when I see the graffiti jacket-wearing guy, but I don't notice any handoff. What I do see is him speaking to the guy Rachel was dancing with over his shoulder. So, they definitely appear to have spoken.

I have my dealer. I have my solicitor. What I don't have is full use of my leg to fucking get them. My fingers drum the manila envelope. I'm almost scared to open it. I fiddle with the clasp, bend it up, and pull open the top. Inside is the police report from Rachel's death. It states, in layman's terms, that her death was an accidental overdose, and the file is closed. The next page is her autopsy report, stating her cause of death was a fentanyl overdose. There were no signs of foul play, no bruising around her face, hands, or anywhere else. No signs of sexual assault.

They aren't even trying to go after her killer. Just another junkie in their minds. Except that's not who my sister was.

Behind the paperwork is a handwritten note from Jobie.

I'm sorry again about what happened with your sister. Now that you know the two people involved, we can discuss the next steps when I get home from work.

Jobie.

We?

I get why he assumes we are in this together. We've spent every moment when he's not working together and have become comfortable with each other's presence. I've even caught him staring at me like I'm his next meal and he's starving, almost ravenous.

I glance at the calendar. I still have a week before I see the doctor and potentially have my cast removed.

I'm not waiting. I remember my sister had a cast on her leg to straighten out her turned ankle. My mom used scissors because she couldn't afford to take her back to the doctors again for another visit at the time. It took hours, but she managed to do it.

I swing my legs over the edge of the bed and yank open the nightstand drawer. No scissors. I stand, slap my hand against the wall, and hop the short distance to the bathroom and lower myself to the floor. The cabinet beneath the vanity creaks open, and I yank out a bin full of medical supplies. I don't know if it's because he's a bouncer who frequently gets injured or if Jobie is secretly a doctor, but he has everything you could need to patch yourself up under his sink. There's even a suture kit. The light above the sink reflects off the funky pair of medical scissors. I run my fingertip over their thick, curved blades and smile. These will work.

The first cut is easy, right on the edge by my shin, where the casting is thin. But the next one nearly kills me. This is more difficult than I thought. No wonder my mom was sweating by the time my sister's foot broke free from its prison.

My fingers redden and burn as I press on, forcing the blades further and further through the cast. After what feels like forever, I stop cutting and turn my leg sideways. My eyes widen, and I sigh. I'm only a quarter of the way down my leg. A blister forms between my fingers, the constant friction damaging my skin. I press my fingers into my temples, running them in circles, trying to will away the pain that's searing through my head. Bits of cast litter the floor around me. I swipe up as much of it as I can and drop it in the trash before picking up the scissors and beginning again. Rain pings against the bathroom window. I turn my head and stare at a droplet, watching it as it joins another and races down the pane. I plant my tongue between my teeth, determination forcing me to focus and work on the task at hand.

After several painful minutes, maybe even an hour, I finally reach my ankle. I drop the scissors and grab either side of the cast, pushing hard. It doesn't budge. I need to get around the corner. I seize the scissors tightly, ignoring the pain in my finger, and put everything I have left in me into getting through this last little bit. When I cut through the bottom, the cast slides off. I wrinkle my nose and pinch my nostrils.

Good God, I remember that smell from when my sister had hers removed. Funky, unclean leg with a side of unwashed, dead skin. Blech. I toss the broken cast piece in the trash, knocking it over. The hell with it. He's going to be mad when he comes home to find me gone anyway. The garbage can mess I leave on the floor is the least of my problems. I grip the sink tight and pull myself to a stand. When I put a little weight on my leg, it feels okay, so I take a step toward the tub. I drop to the floor at once, my leg shaking, painful, and weak from lack of use.

"Fuck," I yell at the ceiling as I sit on my bottom and rock back and forth, holding my useless appendage. "Come on," I shout, slapping the floor with my palms.

A quiet giggle startles me, and I look up to see Jobie leaning against the door frame with his arms crossed. "You know, I have a

Dremel. If you had just waited until I came back, I could have taken it off for you."

"Fuck you," I say, my eyes burning with tears of frustration. "Those men are mine. When I can walk again, I'm taking care of them. Not you, me." I point to myself, pressing a finger into my sternum.

He steps into the small space and kneels beside me. "I know you want to get revenge for your sister, but these men aren't going to go down easy."

His finger traces the side of my face, and his eyes linger on my lips. I slap his hand away and say, "I have a plan. And before you ask, no, I'm not telling you what it is."

He studies my face, my eyes, and once again my lips before wrinkling his nose and saying, "Let's get that leg of yours clean before it singes our nose hairs off." I giggle as he reaches over me and turns the faucet on. Water splashes into the empty tub, sending water droplets up in the air. I keep my eyes on the rising water instead of his intense stare. I don't want to cross a line with him; my focus needs to stay on improving so I can get my revenge. But damn, he is fine as fuck, and the tension between us rises more every day, and I know he can feel it too.

His fingers slide across the side of my face, shifting a wayward hair from my cheek. He wraps it around my ear, and I pull slightly away as his eyes gloss over and his hand travels down to my waist.

I grip my top as he pulls the hem upward, trying to remove it. "What are you doing?"

"Helping."

His one-word reply sends a tingle right between my legs. Perhaps it's because it's been ages since I had sex. Or maybe it's the way he said it, low and seductive. I release my top and let him pull it over my head. I hug my body, not wanting him to see me naked. Before today, he would always wrap my leg and let me take off my night shirt and underwear by myself for showers.

"Good girl," he murmurs as he throws my nightshirt over his shoulder. His fingers hook into my underwear, and I grab his hands, squeezing them tightly, my face suddenly feeling flushed, my body vulnerable. Heat rises between us as he leans in, his lips nearly touching mine, and whispers, "I'm not going to hurt you, babygirl."

Fuck. My legs tighten inadvertently. I want him so fucking bad I can almost taste the sex we haven't even had yet in the air. If it weren't for my funky leg stench, I might have jumped on him already.

I release his hands, and he pulls my underwear down slowly until he reaches my feet and pulls them off, sending them over his shoulder where they land beside my shirt. The steam from the water floats before my face, reaching high in the soaking tub. Jobie turns the faucet knob off, and in one fluid movement, he hoists me from the floor, and my body sinks gently to the bottom of the tub. The water rises nearly to the edge of the tub as he grabs a washcloth, squirts Drakkar scented body wash on it, and lifts my scrawny leg. His movements are slow, calculated, and seductive. As the cloth slides up and down my leg, I close my eyes and moan. The feeling of having the itch beneath the cast, finally scratched, sends a wave of pleasure through me.

The cloth drops on my stomach, and without warning, his hand slides between my legs. My eyes spring open and flit to his. His face is dark and mysterious, yet his eyes are smiling. My heart races as his fingers slip inside me and move in and out. I pinch my eyes closed, and a throaty squeak noise escapes my gaping mouth.

"Shhh. Just relax. Let me take your mind off the pain."

My pain—physical, emotional, and mental is off the charts, but his presence, his intimate touch, melts everything away— almost everything.

The sound of his button coming undone, then his zipper clicking down, forces my eyes open. He removes his fingers from inside me, stands, and pulls his tight black t-shirt over his head, letting it fall silently to the floor. My eyes widen as his pants slide over his hips and his cock springs free, bouncing into the open like it's been trapped for too long, much like my leg. I pull my legs against my body and grip my knees. I've never seen anything so intimidating before. The only other men, or should I say boys, I've been with were my high school crush and a one-night stand. Dillan was my crush, whose cock was too small to pop my cherry, so I still considered myself a virgin after, and then there was my one-night stand, the neighbor boy who lived a few houses down. Let's just say that he had the equipment, but didn't know how to use it. But it was nothing like this. Jobie is veiny, large, and has a slight curve.

"Don't be afraid," he says.

I take my eyes off his cock, gaze up at him, and try to speak, but no words come out.

He shakes his head and leans over, his massive, callused hands scraping against my bare back and legs as he heaves me out of the tub. I can't keep my eyes off him. He stares straight ahead as he carries me, dripping wet, back to bed and sets me down on the edge of the mattress. I sit up on my elbows as he opens a corner shelf drawer and removes a condom.

This is happening. There's no going back now. My eyes lock on his hands as he rolls the condom over his engorged cock and pulls the end slightly to give his load an ample amount of space to land. I scoot to the center of the bed as the mattress lowers under the weight of his knee. He slides his palm up my thigh before kissing my bent knee gently. "How do you want it?"

My eyes go wild. My inexperienced ass has no fucking idea what he means. From behind, the front, upside fucking down?

He pushes my legs apart, separating them enough so he can climb between them. "What I mean is, do you want it rough or gentle?" His eyes drift up my abdomen and lock on mine as a finger enters me. He rubs my other hole gently with another, and my body trembles with anticipation. I've never been fucked. Both my experiences were slow, sloppy, and underwhelming.

"Whatever you choose, you can't change your mind…" his finger slides out of me and into his mouth. He moans, low and gritty at my flavor before saying, "Because once I begin, I have to finish what I start, how I start. Do you understand?"

I nod my head, relax my body and say, "Rough."

Without hesitation, he yanks my legs further apart, stretching my muscles beyond capacity, sending a sharp pain through me before his cock slams into me. I cry out as my head slams into his headboard and his hand tightens around my throat. I'm both afraid and turned on at the same time. He relaxes his grip on my throat and tightens it again as he rams into me once more, banging my head against the solid headboard again. My insides are screaming, and I swear I can see his cock trying to puncture through my abdomen. He grabs my legs and wraps them around his back before gripping the top of my head with both hands and powering into me again. He's going to break me in half. A tear spills over my lids. The pain is intense, but there's pleasure too. Part of me wants to tap out, and the other part of me wishes for this to last forever.

Suddenly, I'm airborne, and he pulls out of me. Thinking it's over, I heave a heavy sigh, but the look in his glossy eyes tells me something different.

His fingers grip my hips tight as he flips me onto my stomach and pulls my ass up toward him. He reenters me hard and moves fast, his thumb circling my asshole. I call out to him as an orgasm races toward the surface, sending tingling pleasure through my inner thighs. "Oh, Jobie. Don't fucking stop."

His rock-hard abdomen drops onto my back, and his fingers climb over my clit and roughly grip it as if he's trying to stop me from getting my release. The thrusts that come next are deep and painful, like he's trying to send his cock through me so it can exit my mouth. "Jobie," I scream his name. And before the word 'stop' bursts from my lips, my body responds to his, flooding him with my pleasure as he relaxes behind me, his cock softening with his release. He lets me go, and I fall hard to the mattress.

Our heavy panting drowns out the rain and thunder raging in the background. His lips press against my low back, tenderly, before he says, "You're fucking amazing." The loud snap of the condom pulling off his cock brings a smile to my face.

I can't talk. I can barely breathe or move. My body feels like the weight of an elephant is sitting on my back. All the pain in my leg, mind, and heart has gravitated into my ravaged vagina. Which is something I didn't know I needed until now.

Chapter Seven
The Way Back

For the next few weeks, Jobie helps me regain my strength. He printed off some sheets with exercises that I can do on my own when he's at work. We haven't had sex again since the night he nearly ripped me in half. Perhaps it was a one-time thing. I'm disappointed some days, and others, I welcome the time to focus on healing.

What he doesn't know is that I have not only been working on my exercises, but I've been perfecting my plan. Through our many intimate conversations over the last several weeks, I've discussed my past and family. Although he didn't share much, he did reveal to me that he has a private security job servicing a wealthy client when they are in town. Tonight, there's a fancy gala he'll be at for hours, which gives me the perfect opportunity to sneak away. That is, if I can keep him from sending me to my room. He only lets me roam free when he's home, but when he's gone, he says he wants me protected. I get it, he still thinks Rachel's killer will come after me. In my opinion, the threat has passed.

I sink into the couch cushion, cover myself with a blanket, and power on the television. He exits the bedroom wearing a suit and tie, gun holster peeking out of the inside of his jacket. "Don't you look fancy," I say with a smile.

He leans over me, takes the remote from my hand and kisses my forehead. "Come on, let's get you in the safe room."

I frown as the television goes black. "Come on, you know I'm not going anywhere. Besides, you've heard nothing, seen nothing for weeks. There's been no threats, no discussion about me, nothing. No one is looking for me anymore. Can't I just relax on the couch and watch Lifetime like a normal person?"

Or girlfriend? Maybe if he thinks we are in a relationship, he'll let his guard down a little. It's worth a try.

"Or should I say, girlfriend?"

Calling me his girlfriend brightens his eyes. I don't think he thought of us in that way, but when I say it, it seems to put a spring in his step as he rounds the couch and sits across from me. "Listen to me carefully, Liv. I've been waiting for you to bring up our relationship, and now that you have, there's something you need to understand."

Oh, boy. Here we go. He's secretly married, has five kids, and is already in a relationship. What is it?

"Just like when we had sex, I gave you a choice. If you decide to be with me, I'm all in, but there's no going back. You can't feel the weight of being mine and dealing with everything, good or bad, that comes with being a part of my life and decide you don't want it. Once you're in, you're in. Understand?"

I smile broadly at him. "Oh, I'm totally in." I will say anything to stay on this fucking couch.

He stands from his chair, removes his jacket and rests it neatly over the coffee table, approaching me slowly.

"What are you doing? Don't you have to go?" I ask as he unbuttons his pants and unzips his fly.

"I have a little time," he says, glancing at his watch before locking eyes with me. "Not much, so it will need to be quick."

I stand from the couch, my tank top pressing into his clean white shirt, my eyes never leaving his, my hand skimming the front of his stiff cock. "If I can stay out here and watch the documentary I started, I'll let you fuck me as rough as you like."

He brushes a wayward hair behind my ear, slides his fingers behind my neck, and grips it hard before planting a harsh kiss on my lips. The metallic taste in my mouth almost makes me reconsider as he says, "Let me grab some protection."

I grip his arm and yank him back in front of me. "No. I want it raw. I want you, fucking raw." I push my hands down the front of his pants and grip his cock, stroking it hard and tight. "I want you to fuck me from behind." The more I talk, the harder he gets; his breathing is growing and rapid. "And cum on my ass."

His hands tighten around mine, pull my hand out of his pants, and he flips me around, shoving me hard, face-first onto the couch. He guides my knees forward until they press against the back of the couch cushion. "You want it raw, I'm going to fucking give it to you raw. But I'm not pulling out, you're going to take my fucking load, deep inside you. I want it dripping out of you for weeks."

My underwear tears away from my body with a quick yank of his hand, and my body lifts from the couch as he forces his cock inside me, his hands wrapped around my throat from behind. His thrusts are violent, almost unbearable. He releases my throat, and I take a gasping breath as his palms clench my waist, pulling me back into him harder, faster, desperate. I grip the back of the couch, trying to keep him from sending me over the back of it as a rush of fluids fills my insides. Quick, painful, and messy.

He kisses my upper back before resting his forehead against it. "You're mine now, Liv."

There's something dark in his tone that makes me hesitate. His words felt possessive and dangerous, like what you'd hear from a stalker who has finally kidnapped his victim and made her his.

I reach behind me and grip his head, tangling his hair in my fingers. "And you're mine," I say, my tone matching his with equal malevolence. "If you ever hurt me, I'll fucking kill you," I say, taking things a step further.

He pulls away from me, turns me around, and straddles my body, his face inches from mine, the weight of his body pinning me to the couch. His thumb grazes across my bottom lip as he gazes deep into my eyes and whispers, "Same." His eyes follow his hand as it traces down my neck and grips my neck gently before looking back at me. "Same."

My pussy twitches, and something wet slides out of me, his load making an inconvenient exit. "Umm, I think your load just dropped in between the cushions of the couch."

A nasally laugh escapes him, and a playful side smile spreads into a full-on grin. "Well…" He climbs off my lap, stuffs his cock into his dress pants, and zips his fly. "I guess you'd better clean it."

His phone pings, and he pulls it from his jacket pocket and glances at the screen. "Shit. The limo is here. Clean up and watch your documentary. You've earned it."

Inside, I'm screaming with excitement. Finally, alone and free.

I stand, wrap my arms around his neck, and balance on my tiptoes, kissing his lips. "Be careful." Another blob lands on my foot, and I frown down at it. Jobie peers at the shiny slime that once belonged to him and says, "That's a lot. Don't hurt yourself cleaning up." He grabs his jacket, stuffs his arms in the sleeves, and says, "And Liv, don't leave."

I swing my arms behind my back, cross my fingers, and say, "I won't." He pecks my lips once more before briskly exiting the apartment, closing the door hard behind him.

Leaving right away was never my intention. I know how he thinks. We've been around each other enough to pick up on certain things. I grab a roll of paper towels and some cleaner from the kitchen and then scrub the mess from my foot, the floor, and the couch. I sit half-naked back on the couch and turn on the television.

I wait an hour, just to be sure, before I stand and race to the bedroom. I saved my hospital gown, so when I wander down the halls, I'll just look like another patient walking around to get some air or exercise. I quickly threw one of Jobie's oversized sweatshirts over the gown and sniffed it gingerly. The musky smell of him sticks to its fabric like stitches. After tying a pair of pajama shorts tight around me, I slip into a pair of flip-flops Jobie bought me and quickly exit the apartment, leaving the door unlocked so I can get back in. My flip flops slap hard against the stairs as I race down until I reach the first floor. Once I'm outside, I find the first person talking on their phone and ask to use it. I call a taxi, and when he arrives, I ask him to take me to the hospital.

Visiting hours are coming to a close, and it's growing dark quickly outside, so I move fast. I ride the elevator to the intensive care ward, stop in a visitor's bathroom, and pull off everything except my gown, leaving it in a plastic bag behind the toilet. I tussle my hair a bit, giving it a disheveled appearance, and walk into the wing where the med closet is. After stealing a medical mask from the nurse's station, I cover my face and shuffle closer and closer to the med closet. A nurse rounds the corner, nods at me, and keeps going. I peer over my shoulder as she disappears into a patient's room, the light above the door illuminated.

I press the buttons one at a time: 1-1-1-4. The panel blinks twice, and the door clicks as it unlocks. My heart skips a beat as I enter the bright room, and my eyes frantically search the shelves. When I find the Abstral, I grab the entire bottle and quickly exit the room. My grandmother had bone cancer, and I remember her bottle of Abstral was always on the nightstand beside her bed. I picked it up once, and my mother scolded me, saying it was a "powerful painkiller" and that one touch could kill someone like me.

Someone like me. I didn't understand what she meant at the time, but age and a D.A.R.E. program in high school taught me a lot. Sublingual fentanyl tablets are potent and fast-acting for cancer patients, but to me, they are my weapon. I grab a box of small nitrile gloves from a wall display and pull the entire box out of the holder, taking it with me. I breeze by a patient's room, stop and peek back inside. Hanging on the wall is a white bag with blue letters that reads "Patient Belongings."

If I go back to the bathroom and retrieve the outfit I came in with, I run the risk of more people seeing me. Changing into a new outfit sounds like a safer option. At least, inside my head it does. I reach inside, unhook the bag, and take it with me to the stairwell. Once I've gone down a flight, I dump the contents on the landing and riffle through the clothes. I quickly put on a Guns N' Roses long-sleeve shirt that reeks of cigarettes, pull on a pair of black sweatpants with a hole in the knee, shove the meds in one pocket and a handful of gloves in the other, before pulling on the black sneakers. I stuff the rest back inside the patient's bag, leave it on the landing, and scurry down the stairs, my heels slipping in and out of the oversized sneakers.

The club isn't far from here, and with the hours slipping by, I need to hurry and find at least one of my marks. I dip inside the alley where my sister was found, the memory racing back into my head, bringing tears to my eyes and driving my hands to do the work that needs to be done mindlessly. I pull on two pairs of gloves for each hand, open the bottle of fentanyl tabs, and shake several onto the back of a pizza box I found beside the dumpster. My hand grips a glass Coke bottle, dumps the remaining contents beside me, and I use the bottom of it to crush the tabs into a fine powder. When I'm finished, I toss the bottle aside. It smashes loudly, echoing around me. I glance over my shoulder, but no one is in sight.

The powder sits in a pile before me, seemingly so innocent and harmless. If I didn't know any better, I would say it was just baby powder. I scoop up the deadly powder, cupping it in my hand and pause, hoping and praying it doesn't seep through. After several frightening seconds, I feel safe enough to close my hand around the powder and hold it tight in my grasp. As I head toward the exit of the alley, a familiar face rounds the corner, his hand holding his crotch.

This can't be happening. Could it be easier than this? He doesn't see me, the guy who was dancing innocently with my sister that night. His back is to me, and his face is focused on the brick in front of him as he pisses against the alley wall. I creep up beside him, uncup my hand and blow the powder into the side of his face.

I leap away from him as he turns his head and coughs in my direction.

"Hey," he says, wiping the powder from the side of his face. "What the fuck was that?" I quickly remove the gloves, turning them inside out and stuffing them in my pocket as he says, "I know you, you're that girl's sis—" he drops to his knees, unable to finish his last word.

He crawls toward me, his hand reaching for me. Is it enough? Did I give him enough contamination to kill him? Fuck. Now I don't know. If enough of it doesn't absorb through his skin, he can identify me. I grab a fresh set of gloves from my other pocket, my hands shaking violently as I pull them on, and remove a tab of the fentanyl from its bottle. When the man falls on his back, his eyes wide with fear, I ram the tablet against his teeth, scrubbing it quickly into his gums before stuffing the pill into his mouth. I remove the gloves, pulling them off my hands inside out, and stick them in my pocket with the others.

I glare down at him, watching as he struggles, as he gurgles, as he fights to stay alive until finally, he stops moving, stops breathing, and an eerie quiet surrounds us.

One down, one to go.

Chapter Eight
The Monster in the Dark

My feet barge along, the oversized sneakers slowing my pace, until I spot someone using their phone on the street. I once again use it to call a taxi.

The driver drops me off a block away from Jobie's apartment building just outside a neighborhood pizza joint. I remove the used gloves from my pocket, drop them in the first open garbage can I find, and continue walking. Once inside, I kick off the oversized sneakers and stuff them in the lobby foyer area. I walk up the first flight of stairs to the second-floor landing and remove the pills and spare gloves from my pocket. I pull off the holey sweatpants and drop them in the garbage sitting outside the first apartment I see. That's one thing Jobie's building does that mine does too. They offer a private service that operates

Monday through Saturday to collect trash directly at your doorstep. So convenient.

I climb the next flight, wearing only the smelly rock and roll shirt and my underwear, and peek over the landing, checking for anyone who may be lingering in the hallway.

All is quiet, so I scurry to his apartment, open the door, close it behind me, and sigh heavily as I turn the bolt lock. The apartment is still and dark, exactly how I left it. I pull the t-shirt off, jog to the kitchen, pull a bunch of random garbage from Jobie's kitchen waste can, and stuff the t-shirt down into the bottom. He only puts his can out every other day as he thinks it's a waste of plastic bags to do it daily. Tomorrow, the evidence of my adventure will be gone with the late-night pickup.

I walk briskly to the bedroom, pull back the blankets, sheets and fitted sheet, revealing the zipper mattress cover used to protect the mattress from spills. I unzip the end slightly, tuck the stolen pills inside and push the gloves in behind them before putting the bed back together. A dirt smudge on my foot catches my eye. It's from my trip to the hospital in flip-flops, no doubt.

The bathroom light flicks on with a quick slap of my fingers, and I crank the shower on hot. I slip off my underwear, grab a fresh washcloth and towel, and set them on the closed toilet before climbing under the steaming liquid. I put my head down, letting the water pound my neck. The face of the man I just killed flashes in front of my eyes. I shake my head, trying to rid my brain of the memory, but I can't stop thinking about it.

He deserved it, Olivia. Don't feel bad. Don't feel sorry. Be happy, be relieved—one down, one to go. I hear my sister's voice say.

I grab the washcloth, balance on one foot, and scrub the bottom and sides of my foot; then I repeat the process with the other foot. My bad leg aches with the effort, sending sharp pains into my shin, but I have no choice. There can be no proof I ever left. After quickly washing my hair and the rest of my body, I dry off, toss my underwear in the hamper and climb under the covers naked. Getting in bed never felt so good. I close my eyes and think about Jobie's words to me. Once you're in, there's no going back. I guess that applies to my vengeance as well. I can't stop what I've started. I need to find the graffiti jacket-wearing drug dealer, but for now, I need rest.

* * *

I wake up unable to breathe. The weight of a body on my back pins me to the mattress, and the heavy scent of whiskey fills my nostrils. My ear stings with a hard bite. "Someone's been a bad girl," he whispers, his voice unsettling.

A part of me is suddenly afraid. Does he know? How the fuck could he? I've been here for over a month and have never seen a camera.

"Only for you, baby," I say, playing along.

His hand slides beneath me, his fingers searching for his target. I whimper as he pushes a finger, then two inside me. "Only me, you say?" He pulls his fingers out from inside me and brings them to his mouth, tasting me. "Mmm, yes. You still taste like us, but with a hint of soap. Were you trying to wash me out of you?"

I wiggle beneath him, but he leans further into me. "No. I felt icky and sticky and needed a shower."

His cock hardens behind me and grinds against my ass. "I like having a part of me inside you." He drags his cock over my ass, his precum smearing over its surface as he traces it down my crevice and pushes inside me. His palms grip my shoulders, and he holds them firm as he pumps himself gently inside me, in and out, slow and smooth. I reach behind me and grip his hair, pulling it. "Harder."

"No," he murmurs, releasing my shoulders and straightening his arms, his rhythm gaining speed but not strength.

He's making love to me. I grip the end of the mattress and match his motions, but he stops suddenly and pulls out of me.

"What's the matter?" I ask as he climbs off me, and I turn over, letting my legs fall open. "Got whiskey dick?" It was in that moment, my eyes finally adjusting to the dimness of the room, that I realized his cock is not only still rock hard, but he's wearing a half mask, like what you'd see in an opera.

"Close your eyes," he says as he takes my hands in his. I smile in the dark, wondering what kinky plan he has for me. I pinch my lids tight as something wraps around my wrists. My arms fly above me, and within seconds, I'm attached to his headboard. I rub the sheets beneath me with my feet, the anticipation making my pussy lips swell.

Something strikes my naked abdomen in the dark, not hard but hard enough to make a slapping noise. I open my eyes as Jobie brings his leather belt down between my legs, the edge of it striking my clit.

"Ouch, Jobie. That hurt," I say, tightening my legs together.

He pushes the half mask on top of his head and says, "Let me kiss it and make it better." His hands grip my knees and pull them violently apart.

I cry out as his tongue digs deep inside me, lapping my interior walls until they are covered in his spit. His nails dig into my thighs, sending pain through my muscles. "Jobie, you're being too rough."

He lets my legs go and sits up; the only visible light coming through the window shines on his face. His glossy eyes are open, but it's like he doesn't see me. "You told me you liked it rough, didn't you? Have you changed your mind?" He kisses my inner thighs and sighs.

"No, I do."

"You said a minute ago you wanted it harder, do you still?" he asks, tilting his head. "Have you changed your mind about being all in?"

"Of course not. I'm all in," I say.

He kisses my thigh again. "So, I can take you however I want?" His tongue drags down my inner thighs and sideswipes my clit.

My toes curl, and without thinking, I say, "Yes."

Pain sears through my shoulders as Jobie suddenly flips me over, stretching the bindings tight around my wrists. "Jobie, I—"

A ball gag presses inside my mouth, and my hair pulls, a piece of it snapping as he tightens the restraint against my scalp. A strangled shriek escapes my lips as he sinks his teeth into my ass, biting hard before diving on my back, wrapping my hair around his fingers and slamming his cock deep inside me. He relaxes and slams into me again, relaxes and slams into me again. "Does this feel like a whiskey dick to you?"

He ignores my muted cries as I thrash beneath him. His rough hand tightens around my throat, scratching my flesh as he yells in my ear. "Answer me!"

I shake my head rapidly, tears spilling over my cheeks, snot dripping from my nose. He pulls out of me, and the bed rises as he stands.

The light from the nightstand blinds me suddenly, and his face is in mine. "Oh, fuck baby. I'm sorry. Am I hurting you?" He wipes my tears, his body swaying to the side. "Fuck. I didn't mean to. Fuck." He quickly removes the ball gag from my mouth, and I sob as he unties my hands. The minute I'm free, I leap to my feet.

I glance at my body in the full-length mirror beside me, and a tooth mark-shaped bruise has already started forming on my ass. My wrists, red and raw, blood smeared in the corner of my mouth from the ball gag strap being too tight and finger marks on my legs. He reaches for me, and I swing, my fist striking him hard in the temple. "You fucking bastard, look what you've done to me."

He staggers to the side but doesn't fall, and his eyes turn dark. "Liv, I'm only going to tell you this once, don't ever fucking hit me like that again."

I slam the dresser drawer open and paw through it, searching for a T-shirt as the fan on top shifts the fine hairs on my arms. He likes the air circulation, I guess.

"What are you doing?" he asks as I pull one of his black shirts over my head.

"I'm fucking leaving."

I yank the next drawer open, and he slams it closed. "No, you're not," he murmurs as he closes the distance between us. "You're not ready."

I laugh in his face. "That red mark on your head tells me different." I turn away from him, open the drawer and snatch a pair of gym shorts he bought me from inside.

He whisks them away from me and frowns. "Liv, please. I said I was sorry." His words slur a little.

"Jobie, you're drunk and out of control. I don't want to be here with you right now." My voice vibrates, and I choke on my words, the evening's events making everything so much worse. The face of the man I killed replaces Jobie's, and I back away from him. "Please, just go away." My knees shake and my stomach churns. I've killed someone, struck Jobie, been hurt by Jobie and bruised by Jobie all in the last several hours. It's too much.

My head spins, and the room gets smaller and smaller. I'm suffocating. My back strikes the dresser as my legs give way. Jobie catches me before I hit the floor and holds me against him as my body shakes violently, an anxiety attack taking over, rendering me mute and helpless.

"Liv, what is it? What can I do?"

His voice fades into background noise, and soon I hear nothing but my pounding heart. Jobie lifts me onto his lap, his arms tightening around me as he whispers in my ear. "I'm sorry, I hurt you, babygirl. I'm so fucking sorry."

Chapter Nine
Breaking News

I wake up in bed alone. The sound of clanking pans carries through the open bedroom door, and the scent of bacon and coffee fills my nostrils, awakening my senses. The television roars in the background, broadcasting the day's weather forecast.

Everything hurts. Not just my skin, my muscles, and my private parts.

Everything.

Jobie appears in the doorway, holding a breakfast tray. "Morning." He rests the tray across my lap and sits at the foot of the bed. His eyes are bloodshot, and his hair is a disheveled mess.

Before he can speak, I push the tray away from me. "I'm not hungry."

"Liv—"

"No," I say, interrupting him. "You've lost the privilege of calling me Liv."

He sighs heavily and rubs his forehead hard, shifting the skin back and forth. "Last night—"

"Will never happen again," I say, not letting him finish. I remove the tray from my lap, set it beside me, and stand.

He follows me to the living room and leans against the kitchen island as I pull the orange juice from the fridge and pour a glass. "Olivia, will you please just let me talk for one second?"

The orange juice burns when it reaches my empty stomach. I gulp it down, set the empty glass in the sink, walk around him, and sink into the couch cushions. My hand wraps around the remote to change the channel when a breaking news report comes on.

"A local man, Phillip Alvarez, has been found dead in what police are calling an unusual homicide. No specifics were available at the time of broadcast."

The reporter cuts to the scene of the alleyway, crime tape strung about, as the booking photo of the man I killed manifests on the screen. Jobie sits beside me.

"Authorities are asking any witnesses who may have been in the area to please come forward."

The number for the police hotline scrolls across the screen. I feel Jobie tense and know he's going to freak out and ask me, so I beat him to the punch.

"You son of a bitch," I yell, slapping him hard in the chest, making him grunt. "I said he's mine. You fucking knew how important this was for me." I storm away from him and yell over my shoulder as I enter the bedroom. "At a fucking gala doing security for some fucking rich guy, my ass." I paw through the dresser, searching for the shorts Jobie took from me the night before. My eyes dart to my right, and I see them lying on the floor. I swipe them up with one hand and quickly pull them on.

Jobie storms into the room. "I didn't fucking do this. I'd never. I know how important this is for you, Liv. I know you need closure."

"I told you, don't call me Liv." I push past him, searching everywhere for my flip flops. My mind suddenly wanders to the hospital bathroom, where I left the clothes and flip-flops behind the toilet.

Dammit.

I play it off. "Where are my fucking flip-flops, Jobie? Are you hiding them from me? Is this another way for you to keep me here?"

He flubs his lips. "This has to be a coincidence." His eyes pan the room. "Did you check under the bed?"

"What?" I stare at him, dumbfounded, wondering why I'd look there.

As if he read my mind, he says, "For your flip-flops. Did you check under the bed?"

Is he letting me leave?

I kneel on the floor, toss the comforter aside, and peer under the bed. Nothing. Of course, there's nothing. I already knew that.

"Fuck it. Whatever. I'll call a fucking taxi," I say, turning to him. "Give me your phone."

"Li—. I mean. Olivia, look, I know I fucked up last night. It won't happen again. I really want you to stay. Please."

Inside, I'm torn. A part of me wants to stay with him and give him another chance, but the other part of me wanders back to my sister and the other person responsible for her death. I need to have closure and to finish what I started.

It's more than that, though, if I'm being honest with myself. The way he was with me last night when he was drunk and not thinking clearly frightened me to no end. I can't trust him, not when it comes to my body or my heart. I need to go home—be free to move about and spring my next trap without worrying about being locked in a room until someone thinks I'm ready.

"Give me your phone," I ask him again.

He stares at me for a long moment before removing his phone from his pocket, passing it to me with a solemn and drawn look on his face. I don't need a taxi, I need my dad. I dial my dad's number, and he picks up on the first ring.

Jobie, what is it? Has something happened? Is Liv okay?

"Dad, it's Liv. Can you come pick me up at Jobie's and take me to my apartment?"

There's a long sigh before my dad replies, *"Of course, kiddo? What's the address?"*

My dad doesn't even know where Jobie lives. Interesting. I hold the phone out to Jobie. "Tell my dad your address."

Jobie plucks the phone from my grasp and, without taking his eyes off me, gives my dad directions. He hangs up the phone, tucks it back into his pocket, and runs his fingers through his hair. "I guess you weren't *totally in* after all."

He turns and walks away from me as the tension between us rises and becomes unbearable. I know I told him I was all in, but I can't be right now. I need to finish what I started before diving into a full-blown relationship with anyone. Not only that, I need time to heal.

"Jobie," I say, following him as he stalks out of the room. "I just need time and space right now. Between last night and now, the guy being murdered, I really need to concentrate."

"I told you last night, it will never happen again. I misread your consent. I should have spoken to you first about your limits before I assumed *rough* meant anything and everything." The wrinkle in his forehead deepens as he pleads for me to stay. "Please, don't go."

He reaches for me, and I step back. His touch and the way his fingers feel against my skin are too magnetic. I know if I let him lay a hand on me, I'll be sucked in by his charisma and intoxicating scent and want to stay. "I have to. It doesn't mean I'm gone for good or that we can't see each other. I just want to go home, sleep in my own bed, and think. There haven't been any threats or issues since I've been here, and you haven't mentioned anything about me being talked about at the club in a couple of weeks now. So, to me, the danger has passed." I pick up a plastic bag containing a few items of clothing he bought me.

Jobie flops onto the end of the mattress and puts his face in his hands. "I don't like this. I'm going to go crazy worrying about whether you're okay or not."

My thoughts wander to the head of the bed and the pills and gloves hiding inside. I need to take them with me. "Can you set these by the front door for me? I have to pee," I say, holding the bag in front of his face.

He glares up at me, nods, and says, "Fine."

The minute he's out of sight, I race to the mattress, quickly pull back the sheets, unzip the cover, remove my contraband, and stuff them down the front of my pants like a prisoner. I hastily cover the exposed mattress, rush to the bathroom, and turn on the sink, washing my hands unnecessarily as Jobie enters the bathroom. He rests his arm on the doorframe, rubbing his forehead with his knuckles and stares at me in the mirror. His dark eyes, seductive and alluring, try to draw me back in. When he opens his mouth to speak, his phone pings. He huffs out a sigh and stares at the screen. "Your dad is downstairs."

I shake the moisture from my hands, stand on my tiptoes and peck his lips. "I'll talk to you later."

His arms wrap around me as I walk away, and I peel them off my waist. "Jobie, let me go."

His hands melt away from me, and I pad barefoot to the living room. I pick up the bag, open the door to his apartment, and leave without another word.

When I reach the landing, my dad gazes at me through the front entrance of the building from the passenger seat of his car. Behind the wheel, my mom stares straight ahead. We have only spoken twice since my sister's death, once at the funeral, where she berated me in front of everyone for getting the fake ID that got my sister into the club, and once afterward to apologize for blaming me for Rachel's death.

Rachel had asked me so many times before if she could come with me, and I told her no, over and over again, as she was only seventeen. A few days after her eighteenth birthday, she begged to go dancing with me, just once. It's not like she hadn't had a drink before. She and her friends snuck into our parents' basement and replaced the bottles of gin and vodka with water. It was the first and last time she drank. She was so sick and hungover, I had to take care of her for two days. My parents were out of town at some four-day couples retreat, so they had no idea their wholesome, do-no-wrong daughter actually tried alcohol for the first time. After that, Rachel didn't touch alcohol again until the night I took her to the club with the fake ID she pleaded with me to get.

I never told my parents it was her idea. I never told them it was all she wanted from me before she went to college—one night, where we could dance and have a good time. We told my parents that we were staying at my apartment, watching movies, and ordering a pizza. Instead, we drank a glass of wine, helped each other get dressed for the club, and went out.

It was the biggest mistake of my life, but I don't want my parents to think anything bad of Rachel. I'd rather take the blame for it all—let them think I coerced her into coming and bought the fake ID for my own selfish reasons. I knew I was wrong for taking an eighteen-year-old to a twenty-one-and-up club, but it was the hottest place in town to go dancing, and my sister loved to dance.

When I approach my parents' car, my dad rolls down the window and nods at my feet. "Where are your shoes?"

"I couldn't find them," I say as I shrug and open the back passenger door. The minute my seatbelt clicks, my mom adjusts her mirror, and our eyes lock in the reflection. "Hi, Mom."

"Hi," she murmurs as she takes her eyes off me and turns her attention back to the road.

She can apologize all she wants, but I can tell by her cold demeanor and the tension in the car that she hasn't forgiven me. I sit back in my seat, my fingers digging into the leather, leaving marks as my stomach tremors slightly.

Not now, dammit.

Frequent anxiety attacks are something I've suffered from since I was twelve. My doctor at the time of my first attack stated it stemmed from the sudden onset of my period at school and the embarrassment that followed. It wasn't a regular, easy cycle. It flowed like Niagara Falls out of me, soaking into my shorts and racing down my bare legs during recess on the last day of school.

After that day, my name changed from Olivia to 'O Positive' for the next few years. I couldn't shake the nickname, not until I reached tenth grade and suddenly had a growth spurt. My boobs came in, my body slimmed down, and suddenly all the boys who once teased me followed me like dogs sniffing a bone.

My father turns his body and glances at me in the back seat. "You sure you're ready to stay at your apartment alone?"

"I'll be fine," I say reassuringly as I fiddle with my fingers in my lap.

I'm not fine, not really.

I tuck my hands inside my pants and underwear and pull out the nitrile gloves and bottle of Abstral. I drop them in my bag of clothes and cover them with my blue tank top.

As the brakes squeal in front of my apartment, I peer up at my balcony. The two plants I have sitting outside look sad and neglected. I'll have to address them later. My dad steps out of the car with me and holds me tight in his arms. "Call us if you need anything."

"I will," I say as he kisses the top of my head and breaks our embrace. I lean down and gaze at my mom. Her locked jaw and stern face keep me from saying goodbye. I stand, turn to my dad and say, "Love you."

"Love you too, kiddo." He rubs my back as I walk away, a tear sliding down my cheek. My mom and I were never super close, but her cold demeanor and lack of compassion toward me shatters my heart more every day.

The moment I enter my pitch-black apartment, something feels off. I flick on the light by the entry, and my eyes widen. What the actual fuck? Pillows are thrown off the couch, and papers litter the floor beside my overturned desk. My laptop is nowhere in sight, and every drawer and door is open.

"Son of a bitch," I say to myself. I reach for my cell phone, only to realize I don't have it. Jobie does. Ever since I received a death threat on it, he's held onto it and monitored mine and Rachel's social media. I still don't know how someone got my number. My parents insisted I keep a landline just in case, so I enter my small bedroom and find the phone. I pick up the receiver and hear no dial tone. I follow the cord hanging from the telephone to its tattered end. Someone ripped it out of the wall.

I stand abruptly, race from my apartment to my neighbor's next door and stop, my knuckles hovering in front of the partition. If I call Jobie, he'll be right, and I'll be back in his safe room. If I call my dad, he'll want me to stay there where he can keep an eye on me, but my mom would make me feel unwanted and uncomfortable. If I call the police, Jobie will find out because he knows people in law enforcement, and they've obviously been helping him, given the extensive information he has obtained about the two men I'm after. Well, one now. I move cautiously back to my apartment. I have to stay. Besides, who knows how long ago this happened?

Jobie went over the day after he brought me to his apartment and said it didn't appear that anyone had been there, so it had to have happened after that.

Bile rises in my throat as I close the door and turn the deadbolt. I've always been terrible about keeping my door locked, mainly because I always lose my keys. Now, it's a must. I enter my bedroom, shake out my pillowcase, and a bottle of Xanax bounces off the hardwood floor and rolls away from me. I don't take them very often, but after the attack at Jobie's and the rising tremor in my stomach, I know another one is coming. I twist off the top of the medicine bottle, toss a magic bullet into my throat, swallow it dry, and drop back into my stripped bed.

Chapter Ten
Always be Prepared

The side of my face burns, waking me up. The sun peeks through the gap in my curtains, sending rays across my face, scorching my skin. I wipe the drool from my lips and sit up, listening to my apartment. All seems quiet, so I roll out of bed and survey the damage.

It's chaos, simple as that.

After drinking a glass of water, I spend the next several hours cleaning my apartment, watering the plants on my balcony, and taking a shower. I grab the plastic bag from the floor at the foot of my bed, drop the pill bottle and gloves on my black floral comforter, and put away the rest of the clothes in the bag before balling it up and stuffing it in the trash. I stare at the pills briefly before swiping them and a pair of gloves and carrying them to the kitchen. I pull out a plastic freezer bag, dump the contents of the bottle inside, and use the back of a spoon to smash the rest of the pills into a fine powder.

When I was little, my dad always said never to put all your eggs in one basket. I pour the powder onto the kitchen counter, slide on the nitrile gloves, and remove a large chopping knife from the drawer. The knife scrapes against the counter as I separate the powder into three piles and scoop each one into a plastic snack bag. I use a wet washcloth to wipe the excess powder from the counter and then dispose of it in the trash.

Killing the first guy was easy, but it was also reckless. I never stopped to consider the consequences if something went wrong. What if he blew the powder back in my face? What if the wind shifted, and I was crop-dusted by my own weapon? I reach into the cabinet below me and pull out a three-pack of N95 masks, compliments of COVID and my desire to one day sand my grandmother's antique desk to give it a fresh coat of stain. I open the package and set one mask next to each plastic bag of powdered death. The drawer beside me slams open, and I rummage through the junk, searching for the safety glasses my dad brought me for my sanding project. I only have one pair, so I need to keep them close to me at all times.

My front door rattles with a loud knock and I freeze. Who the fuck?

I tiptoe to the door and peek through the peephole. It's the DJ from the club. What the hell is he doing here? I'm not taking any chances. I tiptoe back over to the kitchen, hide the supplies for two out of three kill kits, slide a mask over my face, and put the goggles over my eyes. The door shakes violently as the knock turns into a pound. My hand tremors as I pour the powder into my palm and hold it tight in my grasp. "Coming," I yell.

I slide the chain lock into the secure position, rest my foot a few inches from the door, unbolt the door, and peer out at the DJ. "Can I help you?"

He swipes his nose and shifts his weight from one foot to the other. "Yeah, I've been looking for you. I have some information on your sister."

My heart pounds in my chest at the mention of her. Jobie never mentioned the DJ knowing anything, nor was he in any of the photos.

"Open the door," he says, cupping his gloved hands in front of him with a sinister smile.

No.

It's not only the kind of smile, but it's the fact that Jobie never mentioned him to me as knowing anything. And as many times as I've seen Jobie stand at the DJ booth and converse with the DJ, I know they know each other.

"Just tell me what you know," I say, testing his intentions.

He presses his fingers into his temples and huffs as he murmurs, "Please don't make this more complicated than it is."

"Make what more complicated?"

His posture shifts, and he reels back before slamming his boot into the door, knocking me backward and breaking the chain lock. He slams the door behind him, locking the bolt as I quickly back away from him. "What are you doing?"

"The Reaper sent me."

These four words tell me everything I need to know. He's here to kill me. Jobie was fucking right. I should have never left.

The DJ charges me, and I throw the powder at him, casting it across his face like flour. He shakes his head rapidly, wiping his eyes and mouth with his black gloved hands. His eyes grow dark, and I bolt into my bedroom, slamming his arm between the frame and door, making him yell and pull his arm out of the way. The door slams between us, and I quickly lock it and lean my body against it.

Incoherent words filter through the door as his voice goes from loud to garbled and quiet. A sliding noise starts high up on the door and slowly travels down to the floor. I stand back, and a shadow blocks the light from coming under the door into the bedroom. He's on the floor, leaning against the door on the other side.

"Hey, Mr. DJ," I say, the song suddenly running through my head. "Are you dead?"

There's no reply, so I take a few steps back. My mattress sinks beneath my weight as I sit on the edge of it and stare at the immobile shadow beneath my bedroom door. I peel off the gloves and throw them in the direction of my bedroom trash can before hugging my body, afraid to open the door.

I remove my mask and goggles and sit there for what feels like hours. There's been no movement, no sound, nothing. The bed creaks as I stand, unlock the door, and throw it open. The DJ's body falls into the room, dried vomit covering his chin and neck. My feet spread and my arms fly up like I'm doing a jumping jack in gym class, startled and trying not to let him touch me as his head falls between my widened legs. I gag and my stomach lurches as the foul scent of released bowels filters into my bedroom. Vomit flies from my lips, landing on the DJ's torso. I cover my mouth, trying not to do it again, but my body lurches, and a small amount of bile fills my mouth. I spit it on his corpse, step around him, and quickly shuffle to the bathroom. That's one thing Jobie is lucky to have that I don't: two bathrooms. I only have one, and it's in the living room. I grab a cup from the sink, fill it with water, and rinse my mouth.

Barking comes from my bedroom, and I peer around the corner. The DJ's phone is ringing. I jog over to his body, pull his phone from his front jean pocket, and peer down at the screen.

The Reaper is calling...

I fight with myself over whether to answer or not. I don't have to say anything; I can just hit answer and listen to see if anyone says anything. The other option is to let it go to voicemail. As if fate decided, the phone screen reads, *Leaving a voicemail*. I read the screen as the message is left. There are only three words.

Is it done?

I clutch my chest, fear sending chills across every inch of me. He wants to know if I'm dead. My mind reels. Should I reply as the DJ?

My finger hovers over the play voicemail, and I press it so that I can hear the message. It's too quiet to hear, so I crank the volume all the way up and play it again.

Is it done?

I throw the phone away from myself, the remainder of my heart shattering on the floor in front of me as Jobie's voice carries into my ears. Tears burst from my eyes, partly from rage and partly from my stupidity in not seeing what was right in front of me the whole time. That's the real reason he didn't want me to leave: the closer I was to him, the harder it would be for me to see the truth. He sent me both sets of flowers, one to gain my trust and one to frighten me and set up his diabolical plan. If I ended up dead at the hands of the DJ, he would look like the hero who did his best to protect me. My parents would stand by his side, consoling each other in their time of sorrow at my funeral.

Fucking sleaze.

My skin burns as I think about how he hurt me the night he came home drunk. He wasn't sorry, not really. He wanted to hurt me, to make me feel pain. I'm the last link between him and my sister, and he just sent an assassin to take me out. Why the elaborate display? Why did he show me all the surveillance and images from the club? My eyes widen, and my hand covers my mouth as I think back to the photos.

Jobie was in almost all of them—in the background, nearby, or lurking in the shadows. He was always there; he just circled who he wanted me to think was involved. The guy who danced with my sister may have had nothing to do with it, and I fucking killed him. As far as I know, the graffiti-jacket-wearing man I planned to kill may have nothing to do with it either. He was pinning her death and overdosing on anyone but him. I was just a toy to him. Someone he could play with—secretly being the one I've been after all along.

Well, I've got a surprise for him, and he's not going to see it coming.

Chapter Eleven
Blow

After texting The Reaper back from the DJ's phone letting him know that I was not home, I pull my long-sleeved, jet-black dress over my head and adjust my cleavage higher. I apply a coat of bright red lipstick and swipe black mascara across my lashes before sliding into my high heels.

Once night falls and I'm polished and irresistible, I step over the DJ's body, exit my apartment, knock on my neighbor's door, and borrow their phone to call a taxi and Jobie. I explained to him how wrong I was and that I couldn't even stay five minutes in my apartment without missing him and feeling unsafe. "I have a surprise for you." I can still hear his reply ringing through my ears. "Is it you naked on a table so I can feast on your body?"

I hummed a quick *yes* and a flirtatious giggle before saying to him, "Oh, daddy,

I'm not on the menu, you are." I could literally hear the smile spread across his face through the phone.

After hanging up with Jobie, I stand just inside the foyer until I see the taxi pull to the curb. A man wearing jeans and a red hoodie exits the vehicle, rounds the front end, and opens the back door for me.

What a gentleman.

I climb in the back, and he closes the door and hustles back to the driver's seat. We pull away from the curb, and his eyes flit to mine in the rearview. "How are you this evening, ma'am?" he asks.

I smile with my eyes at his reflection and say, "Oh, just splendid."

He turns his attention back to the road, and for the remainder of the ride, we make small talk. My fingers tighten around my clutch, small enough to hold in one hand, but big enough to carry my bags of powder and my last set of gloves.

A slight tremor vibrates through me as we pull to the curb of the pizza place just down the street from Jobie's apartment. I unzip my bag and pop a half a Xanax as the driver peers over his shoulder and says, "Are you sure you want to get out here?"

I see his concern. A large group of men linger at the entrance of the pizza shop, some smoking weed while another stuffs a folded slice of hot pizza into his yap. "I'll be fine," I say as I hand him up a ten-dollar bill for a tip. He tucks it in the front of his hoodie, climbs out and opens the door for me. The minute I fully exit the vehicle, all the men stop talking and turn their attention to me. Their eyes scan my body from head to toe before lingering on my cleavage. The driver stands between me and them, blocking their prying eyes, and says, "Are you sure?"

I smile and say, "I'm sure."

He turns away from me hesitantly, shrugs, gives the gawking men a warning glare, and then climbs back into his vehicle. I turn and walk down the sidewalk, heading for Jobie's. The men at the pizza place make a few comments, but I ignore them. The closer I get to his apartment, the more relaxed I feel as the Xanax spreads through my veins and glosses over any anxiety I was feeling.

A familiar figure steps onto the sidewalk, his eyes bright with anticipation as I strut toward him, the faint sound of my fan club providing the background noise.

Jobie's eyes scan me up and down before he peers behind me. "Did you walk here from the pizza place?"

I slide my hands around his tight waist and grin up at him. "I sure did."

He frowns at me and slides a lock of my hair around my ear. "It's dangerous at night. You could have been hurt or worse."

Wow. The man who just sent an assassin to kill me is concerned for my safety. He's an outstanding actor who deserves an Oscar for his performance.

I slap his ass with both hands and grip his muscular cheek tight in my grasp. "Let's get you upstairs. I have plans for you."

His face lights up, and he turns me toward his apartment. "So, you missed me that bad, huh?"

As we climb the stairs, I lean against him, snuggling close to sell the lie. "I guess I just realized when I got to my apartment how empty it felt. It just wasn't the same. I think

I like being taken care of. I like being your girl."

"So, I take it you forgive me?" he says as his apartment door swings open.

I push his door closed, locking it behind me and stalking toward him. "I do. In fact, I think I owe you an apology."

"Me?" He presses his hand against his chest, continuing to back up as I walk him backward toward the bedroom.

"Uh, huh." I rest my clutch on his dresser. "You've cared for me, helped me get back on my feet, protected me, and such, and I haven't shown you the appreciation you deserve for it."

The back of his legs touches his mattress, stopping him from going any farther. I put both hands against his chest and shove hard, knocking him backward onto the mattress. He sits up on his elbows and grins broadly as I lift my dress above my hips and straddle his waist, rubbing my bare clit on his abdomen. His cock hardens beneath me, and I scoot back, grabbing the button of his jeans and quickly unzipping his pants. His cock springs out with a quick yank from my hand.

He gasps and sits up. "Hey, easy now." I lean forward and push him back against the mattress. "You be a good boy now and just lie there. Let me take care of you." I move backward off his lap, sliding his jeans and underwear over the edge of the bed and down to the floor. "You've done such an amazing job taking care of me, so I thought I should return the favor and do something nice for you." I grip his cock tight and press the full length of it into my mouth. My head snaps back suddenly as he grabs my hair with both hands and forces his cock farther into my throat, gagging me. I dig my nails into his wrists, forcing him to let go. "Don't fucking touch. Let me do all the work, and I promise, you'll have the most unforgettable orgasm of your life."

He untangles my hair from his fingers and drops back on the bed, closing his eyes with a throaty moan. I reach up to the dresser, turn the fan toward us, and bring my clutch down to the floor. I lick and nibble the tip of his cock and let the fan blow cool air over it as I unzip the clutch and pull on the nitrile gloves.

"Oh, that feels so fucking good."

I drag my teeth lightly over his shaft and glide my tongue along its length back to the tip as I quietly unseal the snack bag and dump the powder into my gloved palm before saying, "You want more, baby?"

"Fuck yes," he murmurs as he pumps his hips toward me, rubbing his cock against my lips.

"You asked for it." I blow the powder gently across his cock and balls, scoot away from him, quickly remove the gloves, and stand before saying, "Reaper."

His eyes spring open as I back away from him, and he quickly stands. "I guess you were going to find out eventually. But what's with the…" His eyes drift to the white powder covering his cock and the area around it. He falls to his knees, his eyes turning to saucers. "What did you do?"

I wipe the taste of him from my lips and glare at him. "I killed you like you killed my sister."

He swipes the powder on his cock with his fingertips. "But I didn't buy the Coke for your sister, you did. They told me."

My mind scrambles as he falls sideways to the floor, knocking his head against the dresser. "What the fuck are you talking about?"

"The guys…" his voice trails off. "They said when you came to buy her fake ID, you told them you wanted her to have the whole club experience. They asked you if you wanted to purchase the Dance Hard, Blow Hard package, and you said yes." His head drops to the floor with a thud, his eyes going wide.

I grab his shoulders and shake him. "I thought he said dance hard, go hard. I never said to give my sister cocaine or cocaine laced with fentanyl. I wanted to give her the best dance experience of her life and for her to have an amazing time at the club, not for someone to give her drugs."

"What do you think the *blow hard* means?" he whispers. He shakes his head with a strained smile before mumbling his last words. "You killed her, Liv."

I slam my fists into his chest, screaming at him. "You killed her, not me, you. You fucking asshole."

My arms grow tired of striking his immobile frame, and I sit back on my heels, tears flooding my face. It was so loud in the club the day I picked up her fake ID from some shady guy lingering in the corner. I should have had him repeat it, but I was so enthralled by the quality of the fake ID for Rachel, I didn't bother.

This is my fault. I did kill her. I'm to blame, and I deserve everything that's coming to me. I pick up Jobie's phone from the dresser, dial 9-1-1, and wait for the police to arrive.

Epilogue

My ignorance didn't sway the judge overseeing my trial at all. The facts are the facts. The fake ID and subsequent package I purchased for Rachel directly led to her death. Everything that came after was murder, plain and simple.

The door to my cell slams closed, and I sit on my thin mattress staring at the television through the bars. My case made national attention, making me a celebrity inside prison walls. I'm in isolation for now until I can be transferred to another facility to serve out my twenty-year sentence for the murders of Jobie, the DJ and the guy my sister danced with.

My mom never came to the courthouse or sat through my trial. My dad came, and through a lot of tears, he pleaded with the judge to spare me a lengthy sentence.

The judge stared down her nose over her black-rimmed glasses at my dad and said,

"Actions have consequences, and ignorance in this case is no excuse for leniency." And with that final statement, the gavel came crashing down, sending my life into a pile of rubble.

It's what I deserve. It's what anyone directly or indirectly involved in the death of a loved one deserves. Turning a blind eye to the truth as a whole does nothing to change the world.

After seeking mental health treatment two months into my sentence, I've come to terms with the role I played in my sister's death. I didn't want to believe it, take ownership of it, or accept it as real, but to heal, I needed to face the truth and take responsibility.

I take each day one at a time, but no matter how many times I've heard the cell door open and close, the sound of it sealing me inside every night brings my mind right back to Jobie's last words to me, bringing fresh tears to my eyes.

"You killed her, Liv."

To which I now reply.

I know.

The End

Other books by this author:

Sidero
The Carpenter's Chameleon: Book Two of Sidero

The Unnerving

The Prickling

No One Leaves

Libitina

You Should've Series Books 1-3
You Should've Kept Driving
You Should've Stayed Home
You Should've Stayed Dead

Short stories:

Ornamental – found inside Thrills and Chills: A
Halloween Anthology

Don't Knock – (short version) found inside
Halloween Horror Show Anthology.